EARLY BIRD
STORIES

Bad Robot!

Early ★ Reader

First American edition published in 2021 by Lerner Publishing Group, Inc.

An original concept by Elizabeth Dale
Copyright © 2022 Elizabeth Dale

Illustrated by Felicia Whaley

First published by Maverick Arts Publishing Limited

Maverick
arts publishing

Licensed Edition
Bad Robot!

Lerner Publications Company
An imprint of Lerner Publishing Group, Inc.
241 First Avenue North
Minneapolis, MN 55401 USA

For reading levels and more information, look up this title at www.lernerbooks.com.

Main body text set in Mikado. Typeface provided by HVD Fonts.

Library of Congress Cataloging-in-Publication Data

Names: Dale, Elizabeth, 1952– author. | Whaley, Felicia, illustrator.
Title: Bad robot! / Elizabeth Dale ; illustrated by Felicia Whaley.
Description: First American edition. | Minneapolis : Lerner Publications, 2021. | Series: Early bird readers. Yellow (Early bird stories) | "First published by Maverick Arts Publishing Limited"—Page facing title page. | Audience: Ages 4–8. | Audience: Grades K–1. | Summary: "Rob the robot is misbehaving. He doesn't stop, even when Max and his mom tell him to. With carefully leveled text, young readers can follow along and find out what he does next!"— Provided by publisher.
Identifiers: LCCN 2021001312 (print) | LCCN 2021001313 (ebook) | ISBN 9781728436869 (hardcover) | ISBN 9781728438634 (paperback) | ISBN 9781728437453 (ebook)
Subjects: LCSH: Readers (Primary) | Robots—Juvenile fiction.
Classification: LCC PE1119.2 .D343 2021 (print) | LCC PE1119.2 (ebook) | DDC 428.6/2—dc23

LC record available at https://lccn.loc.gov/2021001312
LC ebook record available at https://lccn.loc.gov/2021001313

Manufactured in the United States of America
1-49647-49575-4/1/2021

Bad Robot!

Elizabeth Dale

Illustrated by
Felicia Whaley

Lerner Publications ◆ Minneapolis

Rob is Max's robot.

Rob brings in the laundry.

But Rob will not stop!

Then he tips over

the trash.

But Rob will not stop!

He kicks the trash.

Mom gets madder and madder.

Max is sad. So is Rob.

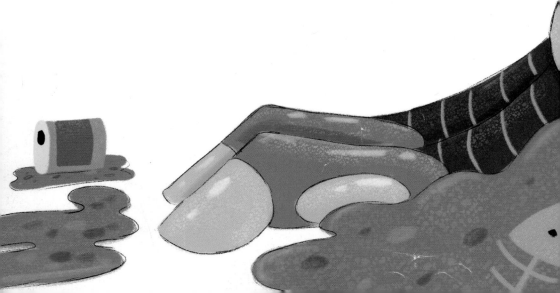

Then Rob sees Mom's ring.

Quiz

1. What does Rob bring in?

    a) The cat

    b) Max

    c) The laundry

2. Why is Mom mad?

    a) Rob stops.

    b) Rob will not stop.

    c) Max makes a mess.

3. Rob _____ the trash.

    a) Flips

    b) Kicks

    c) Helps

4. What does Rob see in the trash?

    a) The laundry

    b) Max's toy

    c) Mom's ring

5. At the end, what is Rob?

    a) A good robot

    b) A laundry robot

    c) A bad robot

COLOR	GRL
Silver	L-P
Gold	K-L
Purple	J-K
Orange	H-J
Green	G-I
Blue	E-G
Yellow	C-E
Red	C-D
Pink	A-C

Leveled for Guided Reading

Early Bird Stories have been edited and leveled by leading educational consultants to correspond with guided reading levels. The levels are assigned by taking into account the content, language style, layout, and phonics used in each book.